BIG CEREMONY

Written and illustrated
BY OZI OKARO

ISBN: 1500411957
ISBN 13: 9781500411954
Library of Congress Control Number: 2014912172
CreateSpace Independent Publishing Platform
North Charleston, South Carolina

To my four beautiful and talented children-
Kosi, Mezuo, Cheta and Arinze.

This is my fun way of teaching you about our culture.

Hi! My name is Cheta. Today my best friend Kosi showed me the most spectacular dress I have ever seen.

What a beautiful dress! What is it for? I ask. Is it a costume?

Kosi says it's not a costume. It's a traditional outfit for her cousin's traditional wedding ceremony.

What is a traditional wedding ceremony? Kosi says it is the way Nigerians are married in Nigeria and around the world. Then, they have a "white wedding" and that's just a regular wedding.

Every tribe in Nigeria performs this traditional wedding ceremony but sometimes they do it differently, she says.

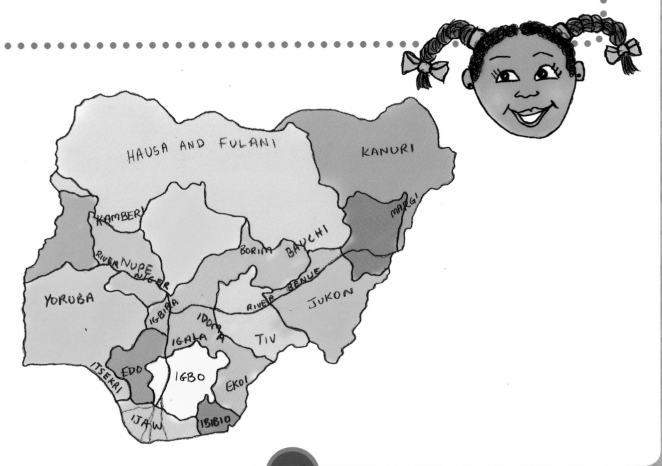

At lunch, I tell my Mommy all about the wedding ceremony.

Cheta, Mommy says, ask your friend Kosi
if you can go with her to the traditional
wedding ceremony.

On our way to school the next day, I was very nervous about asking Kosi.

When I did, she was so excited that she gave me a big hug.

Oh no! That means I need a spectacularly beautiful dress too. What do I do?

Do I need a traditional dress too?

That night, Mommy told me she would take me to a seamstress who would make me my very own traditional outfit to wear.

The next morning I ate breakfast in a hurry. We are going to the seamstress today. Yay!

The seamstress took a million measurements.

I was completely exhausted when she was done. I hope it was all worth it.

Yes, yes it was worth it! The dress is gorgeous!

When Kosi saw the dress on the morning of the ceremony, she loved it!

The wedding ceremony was wonderful.

It was held at Kosi's cousin's house. People showed up in many colorful traditional outfits.

Kosi's cousin, the bride, and her groom wore matching outfits. The women from the bride's family wore the same fabric but sewn in different styles. The women from the groom's family did the same, but using a different fabric. I found out that this is called "Asoebi".

We watched a dance group perform for the guests. I sat with Kosi mesmerized the entire time.

The bride did a native dance. Then she had to find the groom in a crowd of men.

Once she did, she took a glass of palm wine over to him.

The groom's family presented several gifts to the bride's family.

A lady next to me said that in the past, these gifts were called the "bride price". I told her that I would get lots of gifts for my bride price when I get married. I still don't know why she laughed.

There was a lot of food for the guests to eat. Jollof rice, yam, chicken, goat meat, salad and egusi soup. I was stuffed.

When I got home, I told my Mommy and Daddy that when I grow up I definitely want to have a traditional wedding ceremony.

They said that all I had to do was meet someone that I would want to marry.

That should be easy!

CPSIA information can be obtained at www.ICGtesting.com
Printed in the USA
LVIW01n1520180515
438911LV00016B/118

9 781500 411954